Twin Trouble

Peter Bently

QED Publishing

The twins were excited.
"Uncle Billy and the cousins
are coming today!" said Bella.

"Let's go and meet them!" said Bobby.

"Mum!
Can we go and meet
Uncle Billy?
Ple-e-e-ase?"

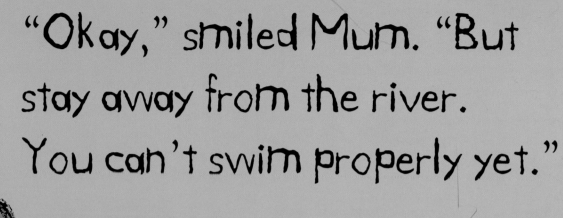

"Okay," smiled Mum. "But stay away from the river. You can't swim properly yet."

The twins waited by some **big** trees.

"Do you see them?" asked Bella.

"Not yet,"
replied Bobby.

Wrestling was
great fun!

"Hold on, Bobby," cried a voice from the other bank.

"We're coming!"

It was Uncle Billy and
cousins Betsy, Beth and Ben!

Uncle Billy and the cousins **swam** as **fast** as they could.

Uncle Billy carried Bobby safely back to the bank.

"Thanks, Uncle Billy," said Bobby. "I'll be more careful next time."

Bobby **shook** himself dry.

"Hey!" called Bella.
"Watch where you're
splashing!"

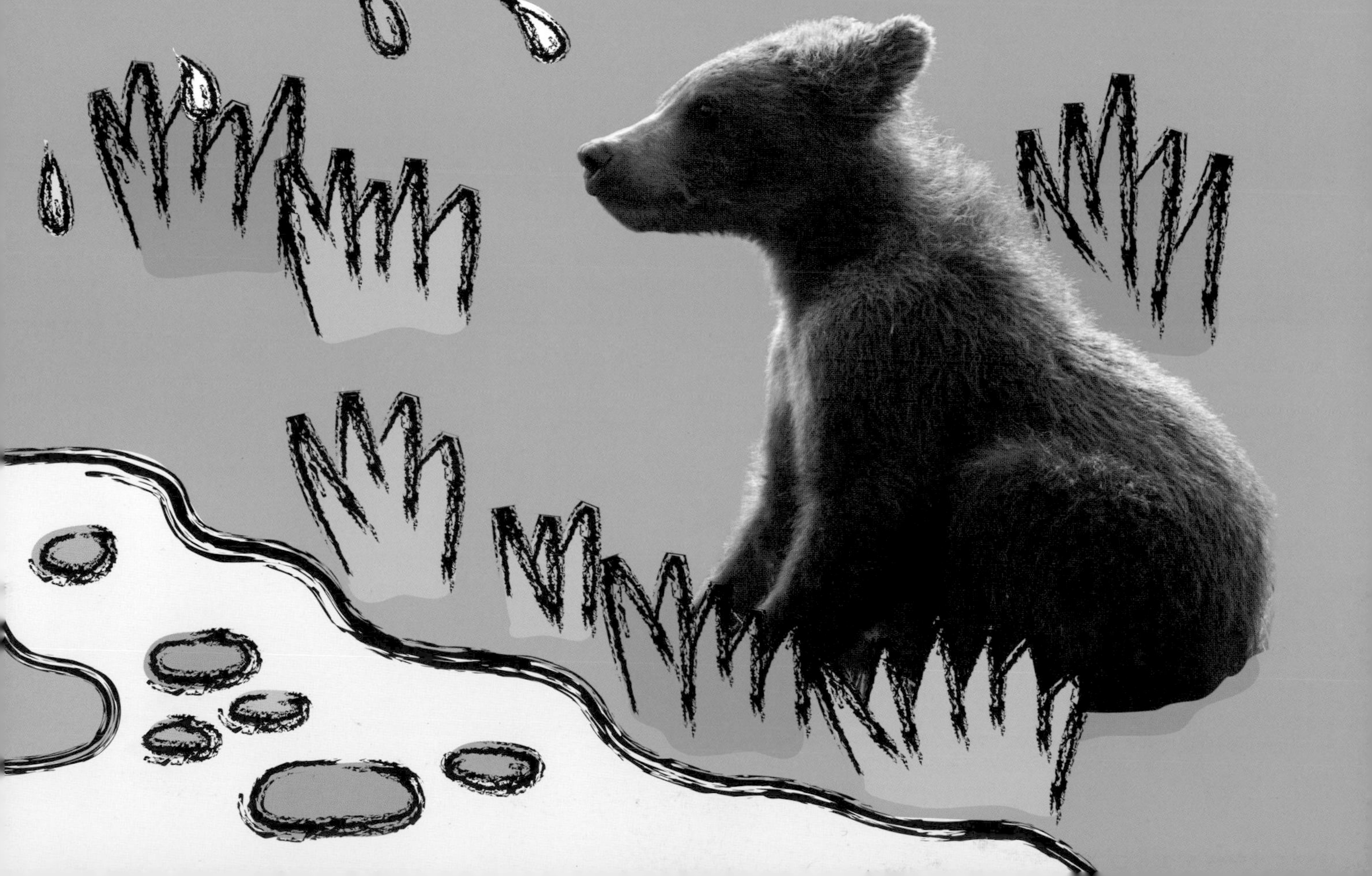

Notes for parents and teachers

• Before reading this book with children, look at the cover and see if they can guess what the story is about.

• Read the story, then ask the children to read it to you. Help them with unfamiliar words and praise their efforts. Can they guess what happens in the end? Which pictures do they like best?

• Have the children ever seen a real bear? Discuss the different types of bear (brown, grizzly, polar, panda and so on) and where they live. What is their favourite kind of bear?

• Ask the children to explain the story briefly in their own words. Do they think it was a good idea for Mum to let the twins go off to meet Uncle Billy, even though she warned them about the river? Are the children ever allowed to go somewhere alone without a grown-up, for example to the local shops?

• Make the story into a play. Two children can be Bobby and Bella and five others can play their mum, Uncle Billy and the three cousins. The other children can be bears or other animals.

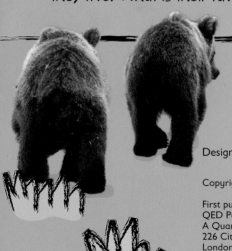

Design and Illustration: Fiona Hajée

Copyright © QED Publishing 2011

First published in the UK in 2011 by
QED Publishing
A Quarto Group company
226 City Road
London EC1V 2TT

www.qed-publishing.co.uk

A catalogue record for this book is available from the British Library.

ISBN 978 1 84835 649 8

Printed in China

Picture credits
FLPA front cover Roger Tidman, 1 Suzi Eszterhas/Minden Pictures, 3 ImageBroker, 4 Yva Momatiuk & John Eastcott, 7 ImageBroker, 9 ImageBroker, 11 Yva Momatiuk&John Eastcott, 12 ImageBroker, 14 Shin Yoshino, 16–17 Sergey Gorshikov, 19 ImageBroker, 20 Michio Hoshino/Minden Pictures, 22 Sergey Gorshikov, 23 Matthias Breiter
Nature Picture Library 6 Chris Gomersall, 24 Paul Hobson
Shutterstock back cover Henk Bentlage